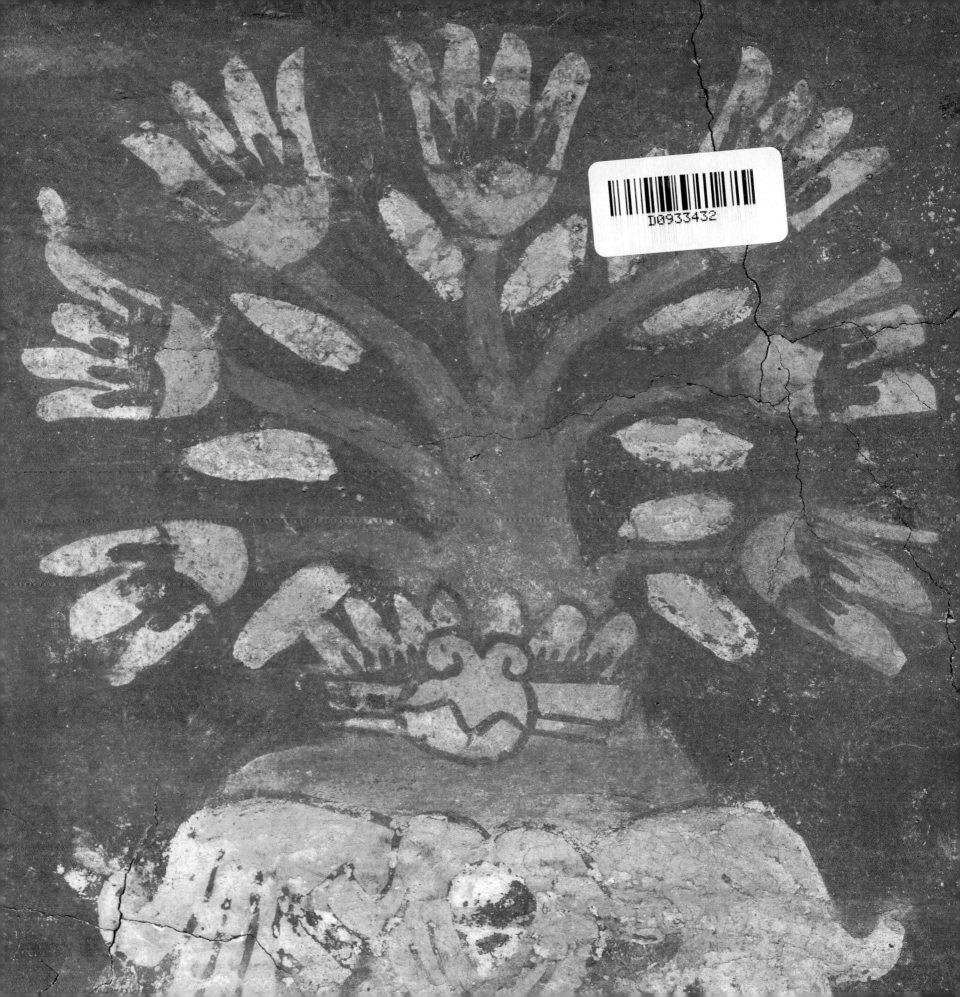

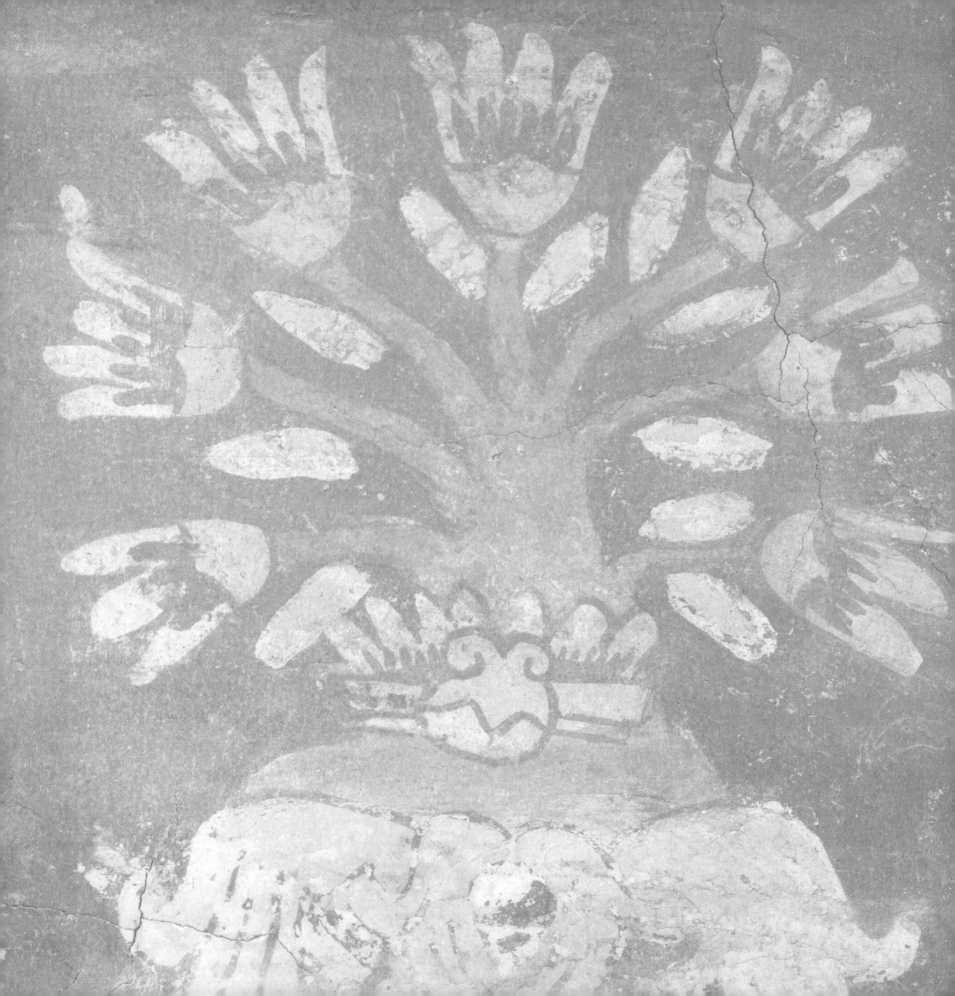

The Legend of MEXICATL

Jo Harper

illustrated by Robert Casilla

Turtle Books

New York

A long time ago, under the blazing desert sun, a boy was born. His mother laid him in a cradle she had made from a mescal plant, and she named him Mexicatl.

In the harsh desert, there was little shade, little food, and little water. Even so, Mexicatl grew strong and straight. His eyes were bright as the morning star, and he was swift as a soaring eagle. He made his mother smile in spite of their harsh life under the blazing sun.

In the starry desert nights, Mexicatl's mother would tell him what her own mother had told her. "Some day a man of wisdom and courage will rise up among us and take us from this desert. The Morning Star will speak to him. He will lead us to a place with water and shade. Then we will live with peaceful blue days and bright laughter."

Mexicatl looked at the vast desert around him and felt small. Who could lead them from this endless sand?

One night, when the Morning Star blazed in the clear sky, Mexicatl heard a wonderful voice call his name. "Mexicatl . . . Mexicatl . . . ."

He stood tall, his muscles tense. The voice rang from above, "Mexicatl, come closer!"

Mexicatl ran to the lofty ground near Thunder Mountain. But, the voice called again, "Mexicatl, come closer."

So Mexicatl began to climb Thunder Mountain. Sharp rocks cut his bare feet, and he almost fell from a sheer ledge.

At last, Mexicatl reached the summit of Thunder Mountain. He raised his eyes and waited, unmoving.

The Morning Star flickered and burned brighter. The deep, melodious voice spoke. "Mexicatl, I have chosen you."

Mexicatl's young knees trembled. He was afraid.

A ringing question echoed through the sky. "Will you lead my people?"

Mexicatl answered boldly, "I will lead. Command me."

"Can you be strong but gentle? Can you be kind but firm? Can you walk with wisdom?"

To each question, Mexicatl answered, "I can. Command me."

The voice continued. "Lead the people southward until you come to a clear stream flowing from a mountain. When you have rested, journey onward by morning, following your shadow. When you reach a place of harmony where the highest meets the lowest and the water joins the land, plant gardens and build a city. There you can live with peaceful blue days and bright laughter."

Mexicatl did not understand. "How will I know the place of harmony?" he asked.

But the Morning Star faded.

Then, in the shimmering moment when night met dawn, a vision blazoned the sky. A cactus grew from a wave-washed rock in the midst of a lake, and on that cactus perched a great eagle with a serpent in its beak.

A thrill passed through Mexicatl's body.

The long climb down Thunder Mountain seemed short, and the rugged way seemed easy to Mexicatl. He did not even notice the sharp stones. He felt only joy as he thought about the vision.

"The eagle is the highest, and the serpent is the lowest," he said softly. "Where the highest meets the lowest is the place of harmony."

When Mexicatl told his people what had happened, many of them scoffed and sneered. "The Morning Star would never speak to a boy like you."

But a few people, looked at Mexicatl's wounded feet. They looked into his shining eyes. They believed him, and they wanted to follow him.

So Mexicatl left, walking southward with his mother and a small band of followers.

The pitiless sun beat them with burning rays of gold, and the glowing sand burned under their feet.

Mexicatl was afraid. Was he leading his mother and his followers to their deaths just for a dream?

Then in the distance, a mountain loomed. It rose like blue hope from the scorching sand.

When they reached the mountain, they found a clear stream flowing. They drank the cold water. They splashed their burnt faces. They lay in the clear ripples.

In the morning, Mexicatl's followers did not want to continue their journey. "We have found water," they said. "Why should we go farther?"

But Mexicatl answered, "This is not the place of harmony."

So grumbling, they journeyed on. They trudged, footsore and hungry, their eyes on the ground. But Mexicatl kept his dark shining eyes lifted. They walked a long and weary way.

At last Mexicatl saw a lake. "Look!" he exclaimed, pointing.

In the center of the lake, a cactus grew from a wave-washed rock. On the cactus was an eagle with a serpent in its beak. When they came nearer, the eagle flew into the sun.

Mexicatl's heart soared with joy.

Mexicatl lifted his chest in pride. He had led his people to the place of harmony.

"I am the great leader chosen by the Morning Star," he told his mother. "I am the man of wisdom and courage."

Mexicatl put a feather in his hair and called himself Most High Son of the Morning Star. He sat apart in the shade and gave loud commands.

From his seat, he commanded some people to soften the earth for planting, some to dig heavy stones for building, and some to make baskets for the harvest to come.

The people began to quarrel.

"My task is the hardest," each said.

"The eagle and the serpent were a false sign, and Mexicatl is a false leader. This is not a place of harmony."

"No true leader would make us work while he rests in the shade with a feather in his hair."

Mexicatl's mother, a shadow in her dark eyes, spoke to her son. "You have set yourself above the people. This is not the way of harmony."

She turned her back and left Mexicatl alone in the shade.

Mexicatl was sad. He could not sleep. "Perhaps I am not a great leader," he whispered to the night sky.

On that cool starry night, he remembered what the Morning Star had said. "Where the highest meets the lowest, there is harmony."

Mexicatl remembered his mother's words. "You have set yourself above the people."

The next morning Mexicatl took the feather from his hair. He went down among the people and spoke to them gently. "Together we will plant. Together we will build. Together we will harvest."

When the people softened the earth for planting, Mexicatl softened the earth, too. When they carried stones, he carried stones. When they harvested, he harvested. Together they lived with peaceful blue days and bright laughter.

The people said, "Mexicatl is a man of wisdom and courage. We will call ourselves by his name."

And they called themselves the Mexicans.

Author's Epilogue

After Cortés' conquest of Mexico, a Franciscan Father,
Bernardino de Sahagún, recorded the legends of the conquered
people and had their writings transcribed. These writings, called *codices*,
are pictographs on fine strips of deer skin. Pictographs necessarily leave
details to the imagination. However, authorities agree on many points.

The Aztecs, who were given that name by the Spaniards,
came from the north—perhaps as far north as Utah. They regarded
themselves as a people of destiny guided by their god, Quetzalcóatl,
who was associated with Venus, the morning star.

As an infant, their chieftain was said to have been laid
in a cradle made of a maguey plant. Because of this, he was called
Mexicatl or *mescal hare*. Mexicatl grew up to be an inspired priest as
well as a chieftain. He led his people on an arduous journey and
founded the city of Tenochititlán on the site revealed by the
eagle and the serpent. There the people began calling
themselves "Mexica" after their great leader.

Mexico City now stands on the site of Tenochititlán
and the flag of Mexico bears the emblem of the
eagle and the serpent.

For Jim, my lightfoot lad — J.H
For Omar — RC

Turtle
B O O K S

The Legend of MEXICATL
Text copyright © 1998 by Jo Harper
Illustrations copyright © 1998 by Robert Casilla
First Published in 1998 by Turtle Books

Turtle Books, 866 United Nations Plaza, Suite 525
New York, New York 10017

Cover and book design by Jessica Kirchoff Bowlby
Text of this book is set in Book Antiqua
Illustrations are rendered in watercolor on illustration board with
some use of pastel and colored pencil

First Edition
Printed on 80# Evergreen matte natural, acid-free paper
Smyth sewn, cambric reinforced binding
Printed and bound in the United States of America

10 9 8 7 6 5 4 3 2 1

Library of Congress Cataloging-in-Publication Data
Harper, Jo.
The Legend of Mexicatl / Jo Harper ; illustrated by Robert Casilla. —1st ed. p.   cm.
Summary: When Mexicatl responds to the call of the Great Spirit by leading the people to a better land, his followers express gratitude by naming themselves after him.
ISBN 1-890515-05-1
[1. Folklore—Mexico.]   I. Casilla, Robert, ill.   II. Title.
PZ8.1.H2115Le 1998   398.2'0972'02--dc21   [E]   97-42222   CIP   AC

Distributed by Publishers Group West

ISBN 1-890515-05-1

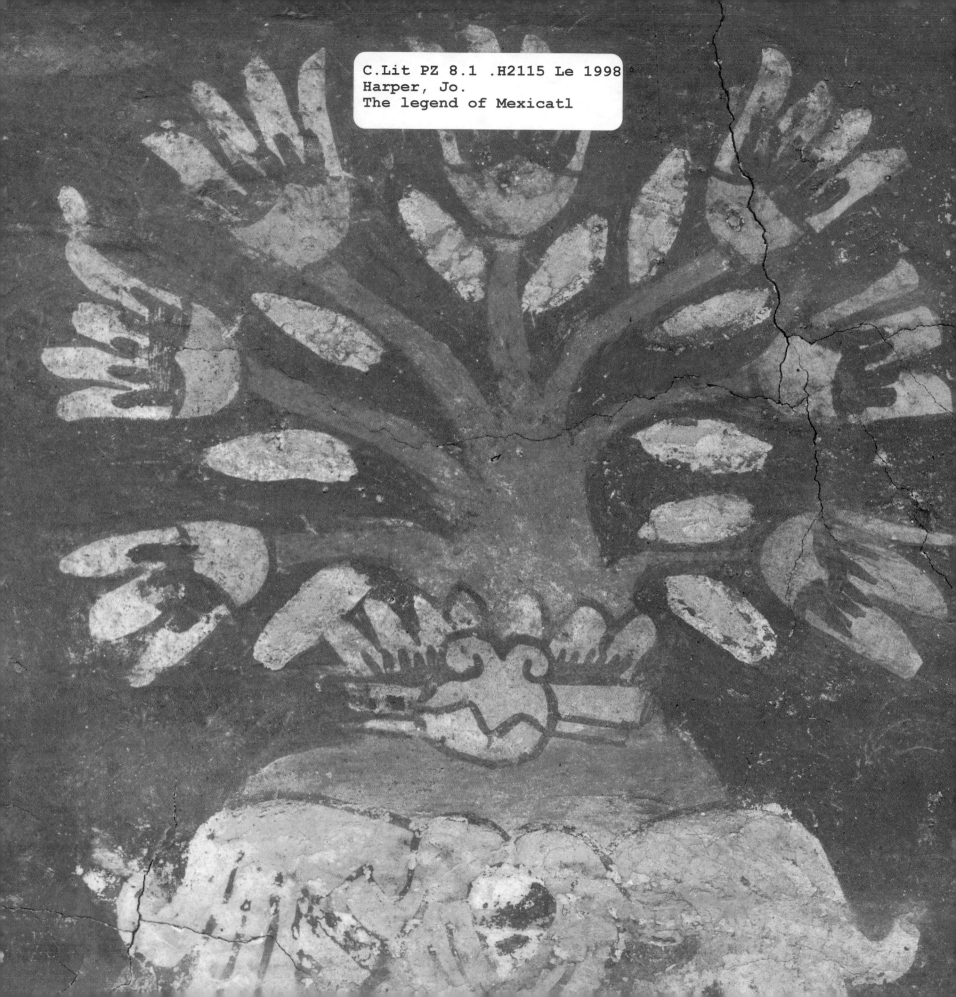